What's in a name?

Cody was so tired that he could hardly keep his eyes open, but he had to ask his big question.

"Dad," he asked, "how did I get my name?"

His dad didn't answer for a moment. He seemed to be thinking pretty hard about it. A funny look crossed his face.

"What's in a name?" he said finally. "A rose by any other name would smell as sweet."

His Dad kissed Cody on the forehead and turned out the light.

"But Dad."Cody sighed. His dad was going to be no help at all.

Cody closed his eyes. It was late. And he really did need to get to sleep. But he had a funny feeling. It was almost like his father didn't want to tell Cody about his name.

OTHER CHAPTER BOOKS FROM PUFFIN

Virtual Cody

Betsy Duffey

Illustrated by Ellen Thompson

PUFFIN BOOKS

PUFFIN BOOKS
Published by the Penguin Group
Penguin Putnam Books for Young Readers,
345 Hudson Street, New York, New York 10014, U.S.A.
Penguin Books Ltd, 27 Wrights Lane, London W8 5TZ, England
Penguin Books Australia Ltd, Ringwood, Victoria, Australia
Penguin Books Canada Ltd, 10 Alcorn Avenue, Toronto, Ontario, Canada M4V 3B2
Penguin Books (N.Z.) Ltd, 182-190 Wairau Road, Auckland 10, New Zealand

Penguin Books Ltd, Registered Offices: Harmondsworth, Middlesex, England

First published in the United States of America by Viking,
a division of Penguin Books USA Inc., 1997
Published by Puffin Books,
a member of Penguin Putnam Books for Young Readers, 1999

1 3 5 7 9 10 8 6 4 2

THE LIBRARY OF CONGRESS HAS CATALOGED THE VIKING EDITION AS FOLLOWS:
Duffey, Betsy.
Virtual Cody / by Betsy Duffey; illustrated by Ellen Thompson. p. cm.
Summary: Cody and his classmates in the third grade are having fun reporting the
origin of their names, until Cody finds out that his parents named him after a dog.
ISBN 0-670-87470-1
[1. Names, Personal—Fiction. 2. Schools—Fiction.] I. Thompson, Ellen (Ellen M.), ill.
II. Title.
PZ7.D8968Vi 1997 [Fic]—dc21 96-47356 CIP AC

Puffin Books ISBN 0-14-130350-6

Printed in the United States of America

RL: 2.3
Reprinted by arrangement with Penguin Putnam Inc.

Contents

Chapter 1

Megabyte

"Killer."

"Frankenbunny."

"Reeses."

Ms. Harvey's class was calling out names. On her desk in the front of the room was a cage. In the cage a small gray rabbit sat nibbling a leaf of lettuce.

Cody Michaels waved his arm in the air. He had the perfect name for the rabbit: Megabyte. Ms. Harvey would love that name. She loved computers as much as Cody did. She let the class type in their computer journals whenever they had free time. When Cody was

on the computer he was no longer just plain Cody, he was Virtual Cody.

"Oo! oo! oo! ooooooo!" he said as he waved. If only she would call on him. *Megabyte, Megabyte,* he thought.

"One more," said Ms. Harvey. Across the room Cody could see P.J. She was holding her hand up too. Her fingers were together. Her arm was bent at a perfect angle. Her black curly hair was tied up in two ponytails that reminded Cody a lot of Minnie Mouse, except that Minnie Mouse smiled. P.J. almost never did.

"Ooooooo!" He waved his hand even harder. Megabyte was the best name. Better, he was sure, than anything P.J. could think of.

"P.J.," Ms. Harvey said.

Cody frowned at P.J. She frowned back at him, then turned to Ms. Harvey. "I think we should name the rabbit Princess."

"Oh brother," Cody's best friend Chip whispered to him. Cody groaned. He looked across the room at Holly. She grinned at him and winked. At least he thought she winked. Maybe she just had something in her eye. He didn't wink back.

Cody waved both arms at Ms. Harvey with renewed energy. Megabyte was a better name than Princess.

"That's all for now," said Ms. Harvey. "Let's not rush. We have all week to think of a name for the rabbit." Cody put his arms down. Ms. Harvey wrote the name "Princess" up on the blackboard with the others.

"Also this week we will be thinking about where our own names came from. Sometime this week I want each of you to give a report about your name."

P.J. raised her hand again. Fingers together. Perfect angle.

"Yes, P.J.?"

"I was named for my aunt, a famous inventor," said P.J. "Very famous." She looked at Cody. "Very, very famous."

Cody frowned. His life had been almost

perfect until P.J. appeared in his classroom. She had been promoted from the second grade in the middle of the year. Until P.J. came, whenever he played Math Zapper on the computer Virtual Cody had always been the high scorer. He had zapped every math fact that zipped through outer space. Now whenever he went to enter his score at the end of a game, he saw the words **High Scorer— P.J.**

When he played Spellicopter, Virtual Cody almost never missed a spelling word. Now whenever he went to enter his score he saw **High Scorer—P.J.**

When he played his favorite game, Pony Express Rider, Virtual Cody raced across the country ahead of all the others. Now whenever he went to enter his score he saw **High Scorer—P.J.**

Yesterday when he went to log on, she had changed his name. Instead of *Virtual Cody,* it said *Virtual Cootie.* He had tried to change the name P.J. to Pajamas, but he hadn't been able to do it. He couldn't even figure out how to change his own name back.

Cody stuck out his tongue at P.J. Surely he was named for someone better than an inventor. He could be named for a prince, or even a king. King Cody. He smiled.

"Everyone get out your English books," Ms. Harvey said.

Cody didn't get out his English book.

What if they discovered that he *was* a king? He imagined what it would be like. He would be sitting on a throne. His subjects would come forward. "All rise," a man with a trumpet would say. "Hail to King Cody!"

"Hail to King Cody!" everyone would say. "Cody!"

He would bow to his subjects.

"Cody! Sit down!" Ms. Harvey tapped her foot.

He had actually stood up!

Cody sat down quickly and got out his English book. He hid behind it and tried to keep his mind on predicates.

Maybe he had been named for a war hero. Someone who had saved others in combat. He imagined that he was in the trenches. He was slipping forward behind enemy lines. He was brave. He was bold. He would save the country.

"Cody!"

He would—

"Cody Michaels, get back in your seat!" Ms. Harvey said.

Cody got back in his seat. P.J. giggled.

Cody frowned at her. He tried even harder to pay attention to Ms. Harvey.

Suddenly he had it!

Buffalo Bill Cody.

One of the cowboys from the Pony Express.

It had to be.

At his sides his hands, on their own, formed into pistols.

"Reach for the sky!" he whispered.

He fired imaginary bullets at P.J.

Pow pow pow.

He blew imaginary smoke from the ends of his fingers.

"Cody? You raised your hand. Do you have something to say?"

He put his hands down quickly.

"No, Ms. Harvey."

He sat back. Then smiled.

Bill Cody—Buffalo Bill.

It had to be. Tonight he would ask his parents, so he could find out for sure. Then tomorrow he would show P.J.

His hands began to form gunfighter pistols again. *Showdown tomorrow,* he thought.

"Cody, free time," Ms. Harvey said.

Cody smiled. He stretched his fingers to limber them up for the keyboard.

As he walked to the back of the room to log on, he walked the bowlegged walk of a cowboy.

Dear Cyberjournal,

This week we are doing reports on our names. I never thought much about names before now. To my mom, I'm Sweetie. To my dad, I'm Sport. To Coach Doug on my baseball team, I'm Number 21. To my friends, I'm Cody. To P.J., I'm Cootie. But to you, Cyberjournal, I'm Virtual Cody.

My real name (Cody) comes from a famous person, a very famous person, a very, very famous person. (I hope.)

Your Cyberpal,
Virtual Cody
Me ————> {:o)
Holly (winking, maybe) ————> &;o)

Chapter 2

Killer Pajamas

"Howdy!"

Cody walked over to Chip on the playground.

"What?" Chip asked.

"I mean hi." Cody sat down beside Chip. " 'Howdy' is cowboy talk. I think I was named after a famous cowboy, Buffalo Bill."

"The guy on Pony Express Rider?"

Cody nodded.

"Cool," said Chip. "Are you still going to be the first one to California?"

Cody thought about P.J. racing toward California on the computer and changed the

10

subject. "Do you know where your name came from?"

Chip nodded. "From my dad," he answered. He looked down at the grass.

"Is his name Chip?"

"No."

"Well?"

Chip paused. "Promise you won't tell."

Cody leaned closer. "Yeah."

"My real name is Reginald. Reginald Floyd Ware."

"Oh, man," Cody said in sympathy. "Why did your parents do that to you?"

Chip shrugged. "Who can understand parents?"

Across the playground they could see P.J. and her friend Angel sitting under a tree eating candy bars.

"Don't let them find out," Chip said. "They use that kind of information against you."

Cody nodded.

"Coooooootie," P.J. called out. "How far did you get on Pony Express Rider?"

Cody's face turned red. She was already two towns ahead of him. "Hey, I see that the cattle are restless today," he called back.

Chip grinned. "Ugly cattle," he yelled.

"Come on!" P.J. said loudly to Angel. "Let's get 'em!" Suddenly they were on their feet and heading right toward Cody and Chip.

"Stampede!" Cody yelled. They ran for their lives.

Cody's arms pumped in the air. His legs churned faster and faster. The cattle were gaining on them.

"Quick, to the wagon train!" Chip called. They veered right and headed for the jungle gym. They climbed in and turned to face the girls.

"Circle up!" Cody yelled. "Circle the wagons!" The jungle gym did not move.

The girls stopped.

P.J. put her hands on her hips. She looked like she was trying to think of something to say. She pointed at Chip.

"I bet I know what your real name is," she said.

Chip looked pale. "You do?" he asked.

"Under." She giggled.

Angel laughed.

Under Ware? Underwear!

Chip and Cody didn't answer. Chip actually looked relieved.

"I said your name's Underwear." P.J. moved closer to the jungle gym.

"Maybe he has a sister named Tupper," Angel added.

P.J. doubled over with laughter.

Tupperware!

"I wouldn't laugh, P.J.," Cody said. "At least he's not named for pajamas."

P.J. stopped laughing. She straightened up and put her hands on her hips. Then she moved even closer to the jungle gym, each step slow and deliberate.

"Trouble," Cody said to Chip. "Trouble at the corral."

"You—take—that—back." She poked him

in the chest once for each word.

"He's not taking it back," Chip said.

"I'm not? Maybe I could . . ."

"I was *not* named for pajamas," P.J. said coldly. "Remember? *I* was named after a famous person. Her name's Penelope James, Cootie."

When Cody heard the word Cootie he was no longer afraid. "What was she famous for, inventing the ugly pill?" he said.

P.J. gasped. As soon as the words were out, Cody wished that he could grab them and stuff them back in. He looked at her face and could almost imagine smoke coming from her ears.

The finger that she had been poking him with became a fist.

The fist came up.

He imagined the newspaper headline:

BUFFALO BILL ATTACKED BY KILLER PAJAMAS.

Tweet!

Ms. Harvey blew the whistle for everyone to come inside.

The fist went down.

Cody's breath came out in a long *whoosh*.

"I can't wait to hear your report," P.J. said to him. "Where does a name like Cootie come from, anyway?"

She hurried to catch up with Angel.

Cody didn't answer, but he was smiling inside. He would have the coolest report of all. He would show P.J.

After all, he was named after the famous Buffalo Bill. He watched P.J. walk away, and hoped that it was true.

Dear Cyberjournal,

How many names can come from the initials P.J.? Pig Jaws, Purple Jellyfish, Perfect Jerk, Pesty Jinx. I'm sure there are many more. I will show P.J. This time I will have the best report. She has called me Cootie for the last time.

Your Cyberpal,
Virtual Cody
P.J. (Tomorrow) ————> 8:-(

Chapter 3

Homicidal Maniac

"Whoa, boy," Cody said to his bike as he pulled up to his house.

A strange car was in the driveway, but Cody did not pay much attention to it. He couldn't wait to ask his mother about his name.

He imagined her answer.

"Well, dear, your father and I looked at you when you were born, and even as a baby you were so brave and bold and handsome that right away your father said:

"'He reminds me of Buffalo Bill. Hmmm. Cody. We'll name him Cody.'"

18

Cody smiled as he put the kickstand down and swaggered into the house. He would show P.J.

"Mom!" he called out. "Mom, I'm home."

He stopped.

A stranger stood in the kitchen. She had bushy gray hair and wore a frilly apron. In her hand she held a large knife. His dog, Pal, lay at her feet. He was not moving.

"Hello, young man. I'm Mrs. Hatchet."

Hatchet?

Cody took one step back.

The knife gleamed. A homicidal maniac had come into his house!

As he looked at the knife, his life flashed before his eyes. Especially the bad things. The time he peeked at his Christmas presents early. The time he told everyone that he could roller-skate when he really couldn't. Was it all over?

"Sorry, God," he said.

He closed his eyes and waited to die.

"I'm from Nannies R Us. Your mother has

gone to a job interview, and she hired me to come and baby-sit you. The interview came up suddenly this morning or I'm sure she would have told you." Mrs. Hatchet put the knife down beside a pile of chopped carrots.

Salad!

Okay, so she wasn't a homicidal maniac.

Cody looked at Mrs. Hatchet more closely. She had a little mustache.

He took two steps back.

Maybe Mrs. Hatchet was not a she—maybe Mrs. Hatchet was a he. And maybe he had just robbed a bank. And maybe he had Cody's mother locked in the closet and—

"Here," Mrs. Hatchet said. She handed Cody a piece of paper. "Your mother left you a note."

Cody read the note. Yes, it was true. His mother was having a job interview at a computer store. She would be back at five. Mrs. Hatchet would take care of him.

Okay, so she was a real baby-sitter.

"I baked you some cookies," she said. She

reached down to pat Pal, who thumped his tail.

Cody eyed the plate of cookies on the table with suspicion. They looked pretty good. But . . .

He picked one up. He looked at it closely. There were lots of bits of something in it.

"What's in them?" he asked.

Mrs. Hatchet smiled. "Chocolate chips and nuts."

Cody took a bite.

"And my special secret ingredient."

Secret ingredient!

Cody's hands went to his throat. Hadn't he seen a scary show on TV about a granny who went around poisoning people?

BUFFALO BILL POISONED BY HOMICIDAL MANIAC.

He spit the bite of cookie across the room. It flew against the refrigerator with a splat.

"My goodness," Mrs. Hatchet said. "Don't they taste all right?" She picked up a cookie and took a bite.

"Coconut," she whispered. "That's my secret, but don't tell anyone."

Coconut!

Okay, so she wasn't poisoning him.

"They're fine," Cody said. "I just had to cough." He picked up another cookie. "In fact, they're great." He took two more. No use making her mad.

"I think I'll go upstairs and wait for my mom." He backed out of the kitchen. "Come on, Pal," he said. Pal didn't move. He whistled for Pal to follow him. Pal closed his eyes.

Mrs. Hatchet smiled.

"Stay," Cody commanded. Pal obeyed.

Cody took the cookies up to his parents' office. He carefully closed the door, put the cookies down, and sat at the desk for a while, listening to make sure that Mrs. Hatchet wasn't coming up after him. And he really meant *after* him.

He switched on the computer and checked the clock. Just an hour and a half and his mother would be home and he could find out the terrific truth about his name. Tomorrow he could give his report.

As he imagined himself in front of his class, he saw himself getting bigger and bigger and bigger until his head touched the ceiling. On the other side of the room he could imagine P.J. getting smaller and smaller and smaller.

She had made fun of him for the last time.

Dear Cyberjournal,

   Today I will find out the truth about my name. Here are the possibilities:

1. Named for Buffalo Bill Cody (I hope it's this one) ———> c|:-)

2. Named for a famous baseball player (Babe Cody Ruth?) ———> d:-)

3. Named for a famous movie star (Jim Cody Carrey?) ———> J8-)

4. Named for a famous person (Pope Cody?) ————> +<(:-)

5. ??????????

Your Cyberpal,
Virtual Cody

Chapter 4

Cody Michaels Rides Again

Cody punched a button on the computer, dropped in an encyclopedia CD, and typed the words *Buffalo Bill*. The computer whirred, and the words *William Frederick Cody* flashed onto the screen followed by an article about Buffalo Bill. Beside the article was a picture. In the picture, Buffalo Bill rode on a white horse. He wore leather clothes and had a beard.

Cody read about him. He was a Pony Express rider when he was only fourteen years old, then a scout and a hunter and a fighter. Cody sat up straighter.

At the end of the article there was another picture of Buffalo Bill. In this one he was standing with Sitting Bull. Sitting Bull wore a full Indian headdress. They looked awesome. Cody printed out the pictures.

"Cody?"

Mrs. Hatchet knocked on the door.

"Yes?" Cody said.

"Can I come in?"

"Okay."

Mrs. Hatchet opened the door and peeked in. "Your mother just called," she said. "Good news. She got the job!"

"Great!" Cody said.

"Your father is taking her out to dinner to celebrate. I'm making chicken pie for you."

Now Cody could smell a delicious aroma wafting up from the kitchen. "We'll eat at five," Mrs. Hatchet said, and closed the door.

He decided that a homicidal maniac could not possibly make a chicken pie that smelled that good.

He ate with Mrs. Hatchet and found out

some things about her. Her first name was Clara. She had four children and twelve grandchildren. She loved baseball. The Yankees were her favorite team. And she had a cat called Sydney.

"How did you get a name like Hatchet?" Cody asked her.

"Well," she answered, "I married a man with the last name Hatchet, so that became my name, too."

"How did he get his name?"

"I don't know for sure," she said. "But I know that a long time ago, people were named after what job they did. Like the name Smith came from a blacksmith. Or Miller came from someone who ran a mill."

"Oh," Cody said. "Like Taylor was probably someone who was a tailor, who sewed things."

She nodded. "So the first guy named Hatchet might have been someone who made hatchets."

"Or sold them."

After dinner Cody went upstairs to his room to read.

Finally, after a long time, he heard a car door slam and he knew that his parents were home.

His father came into his room.

"You burning the midnight oil, sport?" he said. His father always talked in sayings.

Cody was so tired that he could hardly keep his eyes open, but he *had* to ask his big question.

"Dad," he asked, "how did I get my name?"

His dad didn't answer for a moment. He seemed to be thinking pretty hard about it. A funny look crossed his face.

"What's in a name?" he said finally. "A rose by any other name would smell as sweet."

"But Dad—"

Just then his mother burst into the room and did a little happy dance around his bed.

"Cody," she said in a cheerful voice, "I got the job. They want me to start tomorrow!"

She sat down on the edge of the bed. She was smiling. "It was wonderful—being in a store again. It was great to have someone call me Mrs. Michaels instead of Mom or honey." She kissed Cody, and pulled his covers up around him. "Good night, Cody," she said. Then, turning to Cody's father, she asked, "What shall I wear tomorrow?" Walking out of the room, she said, "Come help me decide."

His dad kissed Cody on the forehead and turned out the light. "No more talking tonight," he said. "Early to bed and early to rise makes a man healthy, wealthy, and wise."

"But Dad." Cody sighed. His dad was going to be no help at all.

"Good night, Cody," his dad said firmly. "Tomorrow is another day."

Cody closed his eyes. It *was* late. And he really did need to get to sleep. But he had a funny feeling. It was almost like his father didn't want to tell Cody about his name.

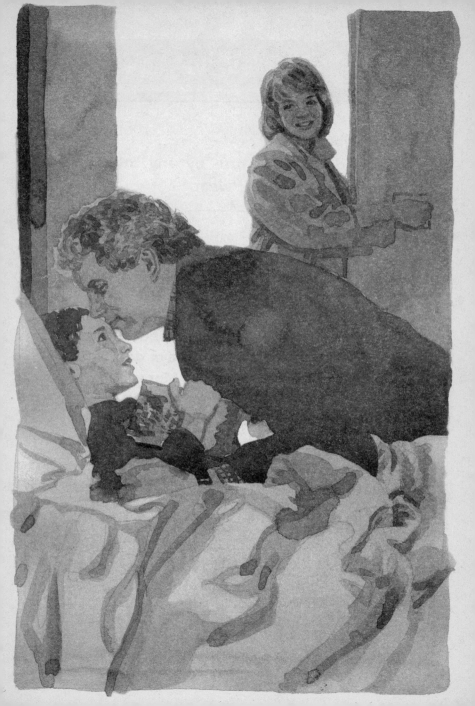

Dear Cyber Journal,

My dad says a rose by any other name would smell as sweet.

A rose ——> @——^———
              ◇

If a rose were called a toilet would it really smell as sweet? Did you ever notice that guys named Butch are always mean. And girls named things like Angel are always sissies. And guys named after animals are always goofy, like Bear or Newt or Monk. Is Mom a different person when I call her Mom? If P.J. keeps calling me Cootie, what will I become?

Your Cyberpal,
Virtual Cody

Me? (a cootie) —————>\\\ ///
                          (@@)
                          /——\

Chapter 5

Madam, I'm Adam

"Terminator."

"Lollipop."

"Mickey Mouse."

Ms. Harvey wrote the names on the board. The rabbit sat in his cage and nibbled on a carrot.

"*Oooo! oo! oo!*" Cody waved his hand in the air. *Megabyte!*

"That's enough names for now." Ms. Harvey did not call on anyone else.

"Who is prepared to give their report?"

A boy named Evan raised his hand.

Cody didn't raise *his* hand. If only he had been able to talk to his parents last night, then *he* could be giving his report, too.

He noticed that Chip didn't raise his hand either. He knew why Chip didn't. *Reginald Floyd Ware.*

But across the room P.J.'s hand was down, too.

Evan stood up and cleared his throat. He held a wrinkled piece of paper and read from it.

"Evan Nave," he began. "Can I use the board?" he asked Ms. Harvey.

She nodded.

Evan walked to the blackboard and wrote his name on it.

"My name is a palindrome. A palindrome spells the same thing backward and forward. A famous palindrome is 'Madam, I'm Adam.'"

He wrote MADAM I'M ADAM on the board below his name.

He spelled it forward, touching each letter

with the chalk. He spelled it backward.

"My parents like word games, and so they made my name a palindrome."

Ms. Harvey clapped. "Very interesting!" she said, and Cody could tell that she meant it. "Let's think of some other palindromes. Anyone?"

Cody thought and thought.

P.J. raised her hand.

"Yes?"

"Did," she said.

Did what? Cody wondered.

"Yes," said Ms. Harvey, *"Did* is a good one."

"Anna," someone else called out.

"Hannah."

"Level."

"Good!" said Mrs. Harvey. Evan sat down.

"Any other volunteers to give a report?" asked Ms. Harvey.

Holly raised her hand.

"Holly," Ms. Harvey said.

Holly went to the front of the room. When she faced the class to give her report she winked. Everyone giggled. Cody's heart beat faster.

"I was named Holly," she said, "because I was born on Christmas Day."

"Cool," someone said.

"Double presents," someone else added.

"Not cool," said Holly. "We have to have my birthday party in the spring because everyone is gone for the holidays."

"Bummer," Chip whispered.

Holly sat down and a boy named Edens raised his hand.

Cody had always wondered how he got that name.

Edens stood up. "My name is Edens Davis," he said. "My mother's name before she got married was Brenda Edens. When she married my dad she changed it to Brenda Davis. She used her last name for my first name. It was to honor her parents—my grandparents."

He took out an old picture of his grandparents in wedding clothes and passed it around. On the bottom of the picture it said *Edna and Hubert Edens.*

"That's very interesting," said Ms. Harvey. "Two-thirds of the names given in the world are to honor someone."

Cody thought about Buffalo Bill and smiled. He was truly honored. He looked at P.J. and thought, *I am named after someone famous. Someone very famous. Someone very, very famous.*

"One more," Mrs. Harvey said.

Angel raised her hand. She stood and went to the front of the room. She smoothed her skirt. She patted her hair.

"My parents named me Angel because I was the most beautiful and sweet baby in the world. They said as soon as they saw me in the hospital that I looked just like a little angel, so they named me Angel." She pulled a small book out of her pocket and showed it to the class. The title was *1,000 Names for Your Baby.*

"Here." She opened the book and pointed to a page in the front. "Angel," she read. "Angel means 'messenger of God.'"

She walked back to her seat.

"That's so sweet," P.J. said.

"That's so sickening," Cody said. He shook his head. Tomorrow he would show her what a *real* name was.

"Free time till lunch," Ms. Harvey said.

Cody hurried back to the computer.

Dear Cyberjournal,

Off to lunch. I'm starving. Here's what I hope we're having:

Hamburger and fries ——> ([) /////

M&M's ——> (m)(m)(m)

Popcorn ——> *********

Pretzels ——> &&&&&

Well, maybe not. But I can always dream.

Your Cyberpal,
Virtual Cody

Chapter 6

Pillow Head

"Sarsaparilla," Cody ordered at lunch.

The lunch lady passed him a carton of milk.

"T-bone steak," he told the second lady. She shoveled a gray piece of meatloaf on his plate.

He thought about getting a salad, but changed his mind. Buffalo Bill would not be caught dead at the salad bar.

Cody carried his tray to the table and sat in his usual spot beside Chip.

Angel walked by and stuck out her tongue.

"How was that, guys—do I have the best name or what?"

"Yeah," Chip said. "What."

Cody laughed.

Angel sat at the table next to them. P.J. and Holly and some other girls joined her.

"Did you get your report ready?" Chip asked Cody.

Cody shook his head. "My mom was busy and my dad didn't have time to talk about it."

Cody remembered the look on his dad's face when he had asked him about his name. He remembered the way his parents had avoided his questions at breakfast. And for the first time, doubts surfaced.

What if he was wrong? What if he was not named for Buffalo Bill after all? Who could he really be named after? Some moldy old ancient ancestor?

Or worse, what if the word Cody meant something awful, like "toilet paper" or "one who sucks his thumb"?

He was suddenly worried. He could hear

Angel at the next table reading out loud from her book.

It was a section that listed the real names of famous people.

"Here's a yucky one," she said. "Marilyn Monroe—guess what her real name was?"

No one could guess.

"Norma Jean," she said. The girls laughed.

"And Alice Cooper," she said. "Guess what his real name was."

"What? What?" P.J. said.

"Vincent."

"Vincent is pretty bad," said Chip. "But for a boy, at least it's better than Alice."

Cody and Chip laughed. The names from the book *were* pretty funny.

"One more," Angel said. "Elton John."

"This is going to be a good one," Cody said.

"It's the worst of all!" Angel giggled. "Reginald!"

The girls laughed.

"That's the yuckiest one yet!" P.J. said. *"Reginald!"*

"No wonder he changed it!" Angel said.

Everyone laughed but Cody and Chip. Chip's face was bright red.

"What's wrong with Reginald?" Cody asked.

"Gross," said Angel.

"Weird," added P.J.

"Look up our names," Cody said, trying to move the conversation along.

"Look mine up first," Holly said.

Angel turned to the right page.

"It means 'holly tree.'"

"How about mine?" Chip said.

She looked up *Chip.*

"It's a variation of Charles," she said. "It means 'manly.'"

Chip's face brightened. He lifted his arm to make a muscle.

"Manly," he said in a deep voice. *"Yes!"*

Evan called out from the next table "Look up mine."

"Evan," Angel read. "Young warrior."

Evan beamed. "Young warrior," he said in a deeper voice.

Cody frowned. "Look up mine," he said.

She flipped through the book and then her face lit up. Cody knew from the look on her face that it was bad news for him.

"Cushion," she said.

"Cushion?" he repeated in a shocked voice. "Like a pillow?"

She nodded. Everyone laughed.

"Let me see that book!" Cody grabbed for it but she pulled it away. "No name means cushion," he said. "You made that up."

Angel smiled and held the book closer. "It's true," she said. "Here, I'll show P.J. and she can tell you." She held out the book to P.J.

"Cushion," P.J. read, then looked up and smiled an evil smile. "Cody's a pillow head."

Finally she held it out for Cody to see. It was true. Right beside *Cody* it said *cushion*.

Cody sat in stunned silence.

"Manly," Chip said in a deep voice.

"Young warrior," Evan said in a deeper voice.

"Cushion," Cody said in his regular voice.

Suddenly the image of his parents at the hospital came to his mind.

They were looking down at Cody as a baby. His father smiled.

"He looks just like a little pillow. Let's name him Cody."

Cody shook his head. That couldn't be it. *Could it?*

Dear Cyberjournal,
    I have a new possibility to add to the list of how I got my name:

5. Named after a famous pillow.

Your Cyberpal,

Virtual Cody
Me? (a pillow head) ——> [;o()

Chapter 7

Aaarf!

As Cody rode his bike home, he imagined that he was on the Pony Express Rider.

The bushes along the side of the road became the mountains of Wyoming. The street became the rocky road of the West. His bookbag became his pack of letters. In his mind someone was just ahead of him, racing onward to California. Cody's legs pumped the pedals harder and harder.

By the time he pulled his bike into the driveway, he was out of breath. Mrs. Hatchet's car was there.

"Hi, Cody," she said as he walked into the kitchen. She was taking two loaves of hot bread out of the oven, and a wonderful smell filled the air. Pal stood beside her.

Cody said hi but didn't stop to talk. As he walked up to his room, he thought about his baby book. It might have some clues about his name.

He found it on his bookshelf. There was Cody's first step. Cody's first tooth. Cody's picture from the hospital. It was full of pictures but didn't have any clues about his name.

Then Cody remembered the picture that Edens had brought to school. Cody's parents had a photo album full of old pictures like that. He had never really been interested in them before. Now he was.

Cody found the album in a box under his parents' bed. It was red leather on the outside, and dusty. He wiped it off with the bottom of his shirt and took it to his room.

He imagined that he was a detective look-ing for clues. He would go through the book and look for the name *Cody*.

The Mystery of the Missing Name.

The pages inside were yellow and crumbly. He turned carefully to the first page.

There was a picture of a group of people in long dresses and hats. Under the picture it said *Aunt Julia and Uncle Barnabas, wedding party*.

No Cody.

On the next page there was a picture of a man on a horse. The man wore leather boots and a wide-brimmed hat.

Cody would have liked to have been named after the man. But under his picture it said *Jonathan Ford*.

No Cody.

He kept turning the pages. Each page brought disappointment.

No Cody.

No Cody.

No Cody.

There were hundreds of photographs of people posed together and separately, arms draped over shoulders, sitting and standing, but none of them were named Cody.

He had almost given up. He turned to the last page, and stopped. Finally, the name Cody. He had done it. He had found his name!

He looked closer. His hand clutched the album tighter. He dusted the picture off with his shirt and hoped that it would change. It did not change. He rubbed his eyes and hoped that he had seen it wrong. But his eyes were fine. It looked just the same.

In the picture was a large dog. He had a wild look on his face. His long tongue hung out of his mouth with drops of slobber dripping down to the ground. A chewed-up doll lay at his feet.

Cody.

The letters were printed neatly under the

picture. Now he knew the awful truth. The truth that his father had not wanted to tell him.

He was named after a German shepherd.

"Are you okay?"

Mrs. Hatchet stood at the door of the room with a plate of cookies and a glass of milk. She put the food down and hurried over to feel his forehead. "You don't feel warm," she said. "Is anything wrong?"

Cody just shook his head and scratched behind his ear.

Dear Cyberjournal,

I always knew my mom was weird but now I have proof. She named her only son after a dog. The question is why?

Me ————————> M
                  / ·· —·
                  ____·

My snack ————> 8=8 8=8 8=8

Your Cyberpal,
Virtual Cody

Chapter 8

Dog Breath

Cody closed his bedroom door, put the album down on his bed and looked in the mirror.

At some point in his young life his parents must have decided that he looked like a dog.

He pulled his hair back so that he could see his ears more clearly.

His ears looked normal.

He turned his head to the side and tried to look at his nose. Was it more pointed than he had thought?

He didn't even want to examine his tongue. He thought about the long droopy dog tongue in the picture and drips of spit coming off the end.

Was it his breath?

He breathed into his hand. Dog breath?

He'd had such high hopes for his name.

Suddenly he had gone from having what he was sure was the best name in the class to the worst name in the class.

"Pizza, Cody!" he heard his parents call from downstairs as they came home. He could hear them talking and laughing, but he didn't go down. He curled up in a ball on his bed and closed his eyes.

"Cody?" His mother came into the room. "Are you asleep?"

He didn't move.

"Cody, is something wrong?"

Cody opened his eyes and sat up, but didn't say anything.

"Are you worried about my new job?" she asked. "Because if you are . . ."

He shook his head and pointed to the album that was still open on his bed. The German shepherd still stared out of the picture. The word *Cody* was still under the picture.

His mother was silent for a while.

Finally she just said, "Oh."

"You named me for a dog," Cody said.

He hoped that she would deny it. *"Oh no!"* he wished she would say. *"That picture is in the wrong spot. You were actually named after the man in this picture over here."* But she didn't. His chest tightened as he realized the truth.

She didn't say anything for a long time but she sat down beside him and put her arm around him.

"It's true?" Cody asked. "You really did name me after a dog?"

"Well . . . yes and no."

"Did you or didn't you?"

"Cody," she said, "it's not what you think."

"Well, did you?"

She picked up the album and looked at the dog on the page.

"Cody was not just any dog. He was a special dog, a great dog, a hero. You know, when you love someone or something, you love that name, too."

"I love candy bars, Mom, but I wouldn't name my child Snickers."

"I loved that dog," his mother went on. "He was my dog the whole time that I was growing up in Ohio."

"So it *is* true," he said. "Mom, you're supposed to name people after *people*. People like ancestors or famous actors or baseball stars. You're not supposed to name someone for an animal."

"That dog saved my life one time. I was just three years old and there was a creek behind our house. My mother was working in the garden and didn't know that I had wandered down to the creek. I fell in, and if Cody hadn't been there to pull me out, I wouldn't be here today."

Cody didn't say anything. He couldn't. He felt like his body was empty of words.

"And you wouldn't be here. All my life I loved that name. How you got your name is not important, Cody," she said. "What's important is that you're here and that you are our son and that we love you."

That made Cody feel a little better. But a dog, even a hero dog, was still a dog.

P.J. would give him a hard time. Third grade was ruined forever. He could see P.J. holding a leash. *"Here, Cody,"* she would call. Then she would whistle. *"Here, boy."* He imagined milk bones on his lunch tray, rawhide chewbones in his Valentine's bag. Flea dip for gift exchange.

Cody imagined P.J. giving her report about the inventor. She began getting bigger and bigger and bigger while he was getting smaller and smaller and smaller . . . until he was just the height of a German shepherd.

Dear Cyberjournal,

It's true! I am named after a dog! How could things be worse? But . . . knowing my mom it could have been worse. What if she had been rescued by:

A duck named Quackers ———> >@//
                                    (＿)

A cat named Hairball ———> =(-.-)=
                              A-A

Porky! ———> ^..^
            (oo))~

Good thing he wasn't named Rover, or Mopsy, or Rin Tin Tin. I think I'll be sick tomorrow. Heartworm?????

Your Cyberpal,
Virtual Cody

Chapter 9

Fleas?

"Hildegard."

"Aladdin."

"Abunny Lincoln."

Ms. Harvey wrote the rabbit names on the board. Cody hadn't bothered to raise his hand. He sat back and chewed on his pencil. He scratched his leg. Fleas?

Soon they would all be giving their reports, and everyone would know the truth. He was named after a dog. He looked over at P.J. and growled.

"Cody? Did you want to go first?" Ms. Harvey asked.

Cody shook his head. "No, I was just clearing my throat."

"Who would like to give their report?"

A girl named Paris gave the first report. She was born in Paris and was named to honor the city. Everyone was impressed, until they found out that it was Paris, Georgia, instead of Paris, France.

Dalila went next. Her name was an African word and meant gentle. On a globe she showed the part of Africa where her ancestors came from.

Trey was named after his father, who was named after his father. That made Trey the third William P. Posey, so they called him Trey, which means "the third."

John was named after a man in the Bible, and Sue Ann was named after her grandmothers, Sue and Ann.

As Cody sat and listened, he thought about *his* report. What was he going to say? He had the picture of the dog in his pocket. He could feel the outline of it through his shirt.

He glanced at P.J. She was looking down at her book. She was usually the first one to do everything. But she hadn't given her report yet, and she wasn't even raising her hand. Maybe she was waiting to be last. He remembered one time when the class was working on a jigsaw puzzle of the world. When they finished, Norway was missing. P.J. had pulled the piece out of her pocket and snapped it into place. "I always like to put the last piece in," she'd said.

Chip hadn't given his report yet either. But Cody knew why. Every time Ms. Harvey looked around the room, Chip ducked.

"Let's see who's left," Ms. Harvey said.

No one raised their hands.

"Who hasn't given their report?"

Cody scrunched down in his seat. Chip scrunched even lower. Across the room P.J. put her head down on her desk.

"Hmmm." Ms. Harvey looked at her roll book. "P.J., Chip, and Cody are left. Who will be first?"

No one answered.

Finally P.J. raised her hand.

"P.J.," Ms. Harvey said.

"I . . ." P.J. said, "I . . . I think we should all write in our journals before lunch."

"She's right," Chip said quickly. He agreed with P.J. for the first time in his life. "You always say it's important to write every day."

Cody joined in. "Yes, definitely. We couldn't possibly have time for three more reports before lunch."

"Hmm." Ms. Harvey glanced at the clock. Then she gave all three of them a long look. "I guess you're right," she said. "But first thing after lunch I want to hear from you three."

Cody looked at the clock, pretending that he could control time. That he could concentrate hard enough so that the hands of the clock would stop. If he thought even harder, maybe they would begin to turn slowly backward. Back even faster, back through third grade, second, first, preschool, all the way back to the hospital.

His parents would be standing by his crib in the hospital.

"*He reminds me of that German shepherd . . .*" No, back two minutes earlier.

He would change his parents' words.

"*Let's name him Jim.*"

There—a nice, normal, common name. If only he could start his whole life over.

Dear Cyberjournal,

Why do we even need names any-way?

Think of how many famous people have done just fine using only one name.

Uncle Sam ————————> =|:-)=

Santa —————————> *<:-)

Elvis —————————> 7;-)

Think of how many characters in books have no names at all.

The cat in the hat ————> ||||||||||||||8^)x

The very hungry caterpillar —> @;;;;;;;;;;;;;;;;

The Cheshire Cat ————>   )

Having no name would be a blessing.

Your Cyberpal,
Virtual Cody

Chapter 10

Ms. Moldy Cheese

"Ima Pigg," Angel said as Cody and Chip sat down with their lunch trays.

"For once we agree," Cody said over his shoulder.

"Angel's reading the most unusual names out of her book," said P.J.

"There were twin sisters with the last name Pigg," Angel said. "Their father named them Ima and Ura."

"Read more," P.J. said.

"Here's a man named Barry Cuda."

P.J. laughed. "His parents had a sense of humor."

"Too bad for him," Cody said.

"Let me see." P.J. took the book. "Apto-nyms," she read. "That's when people have jobs that go with their names." She flipped through the pages.

"Mrs. Screech," she said. "Guess what job she has. Singing teacher," she announced, be-fore anyone could say anything.

"Mr. Crumb. Guess what he invented. The potato chip."

"You're supposed to give us time to guess, P.J.," Chip said.

P.J. closed the book.

"Lots of people have unusual names," she said. "Like Ms. Harvey."

"Ms. Harvey?" Cody said. "That's not very unusual."

"No, not her last name, her first name."

"She has a first name?" Cody asked. He had never thought of a teacher as having a first name.

"Yes, dummy, everyone, even teachers, has

a first name." That P.J. was such a know-it-all.

"Well?"

"I don't know if I should tell you guys," she said to Cody and Chip. "You are *so* mean."

Cody sat in silence for a moment. One thing he knew about P.J. was that she could never keep a secret.

"Don't tell us," he said.

"It's Bree."

"Bree?"

"Bree?"

The name echoed around the lunchroom.

"I saw it in the office," P.J. said. "Bree Harvey."

"What kind of name is Bree?" Cody asked. "Isn't that the name of a cheese?"

"A moldy cheese," said Chip. "The kind they put into caves to mold. Ms. Harvey's name is Moldy Cheese?"

"*Ms.* Moldy Cheese," Cody added.

The girls laughed.

The name *Ms. Moldy Cheese* began to circulate around the lunchroom.

Cody imagined Ms. Harvey as a giant block of cheese.

He giggled. He imagined an entire family of cheeses. "Maybe she has a sister named Limburger."

The girls laughed again. This was fun.

"Or a brother named Cheddar."

"Uh, Cody?" Across the table Chip's eyes were wide.

Cody didn't notice. He was on a roll. "Or a sister named baby Swiss."

Now Chip was making slashing gestures across his throat. *Cut. Cut.*

"Maybe her mother's name is Velveeta."

Someone cleared her throat.

He stopped.

The roll was over.

He turned.

Ms. Moldy Cheese was right behind him, and Ms. Moldy Cheese was not happy.

Dear Cyberjournal,

I called my teacher Ms. Moldy Cheese.

Wait—it's worse than that. She HEARD me.

My teacher's face when she heard me ——> &;-I

Me when I saw my teacher's face ——> =:-o

Your Cyberpal,
Virtual Cody

Chapter 11

Yuck!

"Class."

Ms. Harvey's voice was not cheerful.

They had returned from lunch. Everyone was perfectly still.

"Before our last three reports, I would like to tell you about my name. It comes from Briana. My father's name was Brian. Bree is what people call me. It has nothing to do with cheese."

She looked out at Cody and Chip and P.J. No one spoke. No one breathed.

"Now," she said finally. "Let's put this behind us. On to the last three reports."

Cody took a deep breath and slumped in his seat.

Chip covered his head with his hands.

P.J. looked down at her desk.

"No volunteers?" Ms. Harvey said. "Hmmm." She thought for a moment. "I'll tell you something else about the name Bree," she said. "When I was your age, I hated my name."

"You did?" P.J. spoke without even raising her hand. Her voice sounded so miserable that Cody felt sorry for her. He realized that P.J. must have a terrible name too.

Ms. Harvey nodded. "When I was your age, kids would tease me about my name. Can you imagine that?"

No one answered.

Cody could imagine it perfectly. He had been imagining it every night this week.

"No one here could possibly have a name worse than Bree."

"I don't know." Chip looked doubtful.

"In fact," Ms. Harvey looked at them. "If there was a yucky name contest, I would be the winner. No one has a worse name I'm sure."

"They could," Cody said.

"Maybe we should have a contest," Ms. Harvey continued. "A yucky name contest."

A contest?

Cody saw P.J. sit up straighter. She looked over at Cody. For a moment Cody felt like he could see exactly what P.J. was thinking. She was thinking: I'm going to win the contest. He straightened in his seat too. Surely his name was worse than P.J.'s name.

He wanted to win the contest too. He raised his hand.

P.J.'s hand shot up faster. "I have the worst name," she said.

"I thought you were named after a famous inventor," Ms. Harvey said.

"Well," P.J. said, "my aunt was an inventor but she wasn't famous."

"Do you want to give your report, P.J.?"

P.J. nodded. She stood and walked to the front of the class. She took a deep breath.

"I was named after my aunt, Penelope Jones. She was the inventor . . ."

She paused. The class was completely silent.

"Inventor of . . ."

She stopped again.

Cody leaned forward. What could possibly be so bad? He didn't even let himself imagine. If he did, he might miss this, and it was going to be good.

"Inventor of . . . the musical potty chair."

A murmur went through the class.

"Did she say potty chair?" Chip asked Cody under his breath.

"She said *musical* potty chair," Cody answered.

"Potty chair?" Ms. Harvey said covering her mouth. She looked like she was trying not to let a laugh escape.

P.J. giggled.

"It played 'How Dry I Am.'"

Ms. Harvey held P.J.'s hand up in the air as if she was a boxer who'd just won a match. "P.J. gets the prize. Her name is even worse than Bree," she said.

A prize for the worst name! Cody looked around. Everyone was cheering. P.J. had done it again! She had beaten him at one more thing. **High Scorer—P.J.**

Cody sat up straight in his seat.

P.J. was taking a bow.

Cody sat up straighter.

"Oooooo! Ooo! Ooo!" He waved his hand in the air.

"Yes, Cody," Ms. Harvey said.

"Mine is worse!" he blurted out. "Much worse. Much, much worse!"

Ms. Harvey shook her head and laughed. "Come on up," she said.

Cody touched the picture in his pocket confidently. He stood and walked to the front of the class and stood beside P.J.

"I was named after . . ."

He pulled the picture out of his pocket, held it up, and pointed to it. "Him!"

"A dog?" Angel said.

"Your parents named you after a *dog?*" Edens said.

"Eewwww!" three girls added.

Expressions of sympathy echoed around the room.

"Actually it was a German shepherd."

"Yuck!" another girl said.

"Actually," Cody said proudly, "it was a slobbery German shepherd."

"I think it's a tie," said Ms. Harvey, laughing.

"What's the prize?" asked Cody.

Ms. Harvey looked confused. "What prize?"

"You said P.J. wins the prize."

"Oh, that's just a figure of speech," Ms. Harvey said. "There's not really a prize."

"There's not?" said P.J.

"No prize?" said Cody.

"Aawwwwww!" A moan came from the class.

Ms. Harvey thought for a moment.

"Well," she said, "I know one prize we can give you."

"Yes?" Cody said.

"Yes?" P.J. said.

"You two can be the ones to name the rabbit."

The entire class cheered.

"The yucky-name contest winners!" Ms. Harvey said. She lifted P.J.'s hand up on one side and Cody's on the other.

Everyone was clapping for P.J. and Cody. Cody wasn't sure, but he thought that Holly clapped the loudest of all.

"Wait!" Chip said. "Reginald! Mine's yucky! Reginald's yucky."

Nobody paid any attention. They were too busy yelling for P.J. and Cody.

Dear Cyberjournal,
   We get to name the bunny!

```
                              \\
                             (")
Bunny ———————>               /uu
                            *()()
```

What shall it be?

```
    ▉           \\          oo          @
   (")         +(")+       (")         (")
   /uu          /uu        /uu         /uu
  *()()         *()        *()         *()
```

Abunny   **Franken-**   **Mickey**   **Aladdin?**
Lincoln?   **bunny?**   **Mouse?**

The rabbit needs a special name, like Megabyte. But how can I ever convince P.J.?

Your Cyberpal,
Virtual Cody

Chapter 12

One . . . Two . . . Three . . .

P.J. and Cody stood out in the hall.

Cody looked at P.J.

P.J. looked at Cody. She crossed her arms and then she tapped her foot.

Cody waited for her to say something mean about his report, or bark or laugh or something. She didn't.

Any other day he would be giving her a hard time. Like calling her potty lady. But he didn't feel like it today.

They had something more important to do.

"We've got to think of something good," Cody said.

P.J. nodded. "Names are important."

"Believe me, I know!" said Cody.

"Me too," said P.J.

They laughed.

"Let's give the rabbit a good name," P.J. said. "Like Princess."

Cody shook his head. "I have a better name. You've seen the way she eats. I think we should name the rabbit Megabyte."

P.J. frowned. "Princess!" she said.

Cody wasn't going to give in. A name was too important.

"Megabyte!" he said.

"Princess!"

"Megabyte!"

"Princess!"

"Megabyte!"

P.J. stopped yelling. Cody stopped, too.

"Are you thinking what I'm thinking?" he asked.

P.J. nodded. They hurried back into the classroom.

"I have it!" said P.J.

"*We* have it!" corrected Cody.

"I get to tell them!" said P.J.

"Let's do it together," Cody said.

P.J. nodded. "One . . . two . . . three . . ."

"Princess Megabyte!" they said together.

"I love it!" said Ms. Harvey.

The class called out their approval.

"Great!"

"Cool!"

"Cute!"

P.J. and Cody shook hands.

Everyone clapped. Princess Megabyte didn't even look up. She sat and nibbled a leaf of lettuce as the whole class cheered her new name.

Dear Cyberjournal,

    It has been a busy day.

Today I, I mean we, named the rabbit Princess Megabyte.

Today P.J. showed me how to change my name back in the computer. I'm Virtual Cody again!

Today I got to California.

Today Holly winked at me. I'm sure of it and I winked back.

Your Cyberpal,
Virtual Cody

Holly (winking) ——> &;o)
Me (winking back) ——> {;o)
P.J. (smiling) ——> 8:-)

Betsy Duffey is the author of numerous books for young readers, including *Coaster*; *The Gadget War*; *How to Be Cool in the Third Grade*; *Hey, New Kid!*; *The Math Wiz*; and the *Pet Patrol* series. She lives in Atlanta, Georgia.

Ellen Thompson has illustrated more than one hundred children's book jackets, and her work has appeared in numerous magazines. She lives in Franklin Park, New Jersey.